# Talk About a Family

**OTHER BOOKS BY ELOISE GREENFIELD**

*Africa Dream*
*First Pink Light*
*Good News*
*Honey, I Love*
*I Can Do It Myself (with Lessie Jones Little)*
*Mary McLeod Bethune*
*Me and Nessie*
*Paul Robeson*
*Rosa Parks*
*She Come Bringing Me That Little Baby Girl*
*Sister*
*Under the Sunday Tree*

# Ta

## Eloise Greenfield
### Illustrated by James Calvin

HarperCollins*Publishers*

# bout a Family

*U.S. Library of Congress Cataloging-in-Publication Data*

*Greenfield, Eloise.*
  *Talk about a family.*

  *SUMMARY: Genny is eager for her eldest brother's return from
military service, convinced that he can fix everything—even the
growing rift between their parents.*
  *[1. Family problems—Fiction. 2. Brothers and sisters—
Fiction]  I. Title.*
*PZ7.G845Tal       [Fic]       77-16423*
*ISBN-0-397-31789-1.—ISBN-0-397-32504-5 (lib. bdg.)*

*To my cousins
Arthur and Lillie Draper Taylor
for the gifts they brought
to my childhood*

# Talk About a Family

Genny rode her bike down the sidewalk of Fletcher Street. When she passed underneath the big elm tree, a crisp brown leaf fell right on her shoulder and sat there for just a second before it blew away.

It had to mean good luck.

Nobody had ever told her that being picked for a leaf to rest on was good luck. She just knew it. It was the right day for it. Friday was finally here and Larry was coming home. He was coming home for good.

Everything would be better now, would

be the way it used to be. She and Kim and Mac had talked about it last night before they'd gone to bed. Their big brother would make everything all right again.

Genny turned into the alley beside the one-story house on the corner of Sixteenth and Fletcher and got off her bike at the backyard gate. She went inside, pushing her bike along the narrow concrete walk. The yard looked pretty all the time now, just the way it had before Mrs. Parker died. Genny touched a blossom as she passed the yellow mums.

She parked her bike at the bottom of the porch steps. "Mr. Parker," she called, peering through the door of the glassed-in porch. She knew she'd find him there at his table full of tools, working on a lamp. He was there every afternoon.

"Come on in, Genetta," Mr. Parker said. He glanced up at her and went right back to the little lamp he was working on. "Didn't think I'd see you today. I ran into your mother on her way to work this morning when I was taking my walk, and you know how slow she always talks—well, this morning she was talking a mile a minute. All about Larry."

"That's what she's home doing now," Genny said. "She said she talked so much at the five-and-ten, she could hardly wait on people." Genny laughed, thinking about her mother's excitement and her own. "I know we're going to jump all over him."

"Probably knock the poor guy down," Mr. Parker said. "How long has it been now, since he was home?"

"Thirteen months and nine days!" Genny said. "The army didn't even let him come home last Christmas, he was so far away."

"That's a heck of a long time," Mr. Parker said, picking up a small pair of pliers from the table.

Genny watched as he pulled a wire through the base of the lamp. He always looked funny when he worked on a little one. He was so big, and the little lamps made him look even bigger. Just the way he looked when his daughter brought his grandbaby over and Mr. Parker bear-hugged him in his great big arms.

"Something's hanging in the air," Mr. Parker said suddenly.

Genny looked up. "What?" she said. "I don't see anything."

"You can't see a question," Mr. Parker said. "You just feel it." He stopped working and looked at her. "What did you want to ask me?"

"Uh, well . . ." Genny started slowly, wishing he would stop looking at her. "Well . . . can me and Mac and Kim have a party for Larry tomorrow in your yard? We wouldn't mess it up."

"Sounds like fun to me," Mr. Parker said.

"We can?" Genny asked. "You don't mind? Mama said I'm always worrying you about something."

"You tell Edie James I said not a bit," Mr. Parker said. "You don't worry me one bit. We're buddies. Anyway, there's nobody here but me and that room full of lamps back there, and I get tired of talking to other people's broken lamps. Besides, that yard is just as much yours as it is mine."

Genny smiled inside herself because she knew what he was going to say, and she liked to hear him say it.

"I sat around here for months, feeling sorry for myself," he said, starting to work again, "shaming Minnie, letting the weeds grow up and bully her flowers. Then that day you stood right there looking out the door, and you said, 'Mr. Parker, I'll help you do the yard.' That's the way you said it—'I'll help you do the yard.' And we did it up, too, didn't we, Genetta? It's a good place to have a party."

On the way home, Genny rode back past the elm tree and remembered the leaf that had fallen on her shoulder. Everything was going right. Talk about a good day, this was it.

This evening, her father would come home from whatever building or road he was helping to build, and they would all know not to talk to him too much at first. But halfway through his shower, they would hear him start to sing. Loud. Too loud. And she and Kim would giggle.

Then, after dinner, Kim would tell them some new jokes she had made up. And her father would keep looking at the clock. And her mother would try to keep her mind on the crossword puzzle. And Mac would just hang around trying not to act excited.

And then, after a while, it would be time for Larry.

Genny made her bike zigzag down the street—not for any reason, just because she was so happy she felt like doing something. She hoped she wasn't running over any ants. She wanted everything and everybody to have a good day.

But the minute she walked into her house, she forgot all about the good luck. Her father was home early, which meant that his job had ended. Early Monday morning, almost before it got light, he would have to go downtown and stand outdoors with all the other men who hoped to get picked for a job.

Right now, though, Mr. James was standing on one side of the room and Mrs. James was standing on the other, and Genny could feel their anger in the quiet. She could see their anger too, could see it in the tiny drops of sweat on her mother's nose and in the way her father's chest moved up and down.

They had been fighting again, fighting with words, and they were trying to hide it. They smiled too much, and both of them talked at the same time.

"Can you have the party?"

"What did Parker say?"

Genny leaned her bike against the wall and her mother didn't stop her. "He said it's okay, we can have it," Genny said. "Now we'll have enough room to invite everybody."

She knew *she* was smiling too much too. And if there had been two of her, both of her would have been talking at the same time. But she really didn't want to talk at all. Or smile. She was angry with her mother and father for being angry with each other, and for taking away her good-luck day.

"Kim upstairs?" she asked. She knew the answer before her mother nodded. Every time her mother and father had a fight, Kim locked herself in the bedroom and drew pictures on her big white drawing pad. And that was where Genny found her.

At first, Kim wouldn't let her in.

"Open the door, Kim," Genny said. "It's my room too, open the door."

As soon as Genny saw Kim's lips pushed up toward her nose, she knew that Kim wouldn't care about the party, but Genny tried to talk to her anyway.

"It's almost time for Larry," she said.

"I know it!" Kim said. She turned her back to Genny and began to draw.

"Why you mad at me?" Genny said. "I didn't do anything."

Kim didn't answer and Genny sat down on the bed. "I hope everybody can come to the party," she said softly. She wasn't talking to Kim. She was talking to herself.

A picture from another party passed through her mind. Her eighth birthday. Her father and mother each giving two kisses. One to her and one to each other.

She didn't want to think about that right now. She would be glad when Mac got home from his after-school job. He would be happy about the good news, and then she could be happy again too.

It was after dinner when Mac got home and he was hungry even though, Genny knew, he had already eaten at the carry-out place where he worked. She sat in the kitchen with him while he ate again.

"Hey, that's all right!" he said about the party. He sat sideways in the chair so that his long legs were not under the table. With his free hand he rubbed at one of the sideburns he was trying to grow. "I know Skeeter's mother will let us use her folding chairs, and I can get some of my boys to help me set them up. Soon as I finish eating, I'll start calling up people."

"I'll pick out the good records," Genny said.

And that was what she was doing half an hour later when she heard Larry's special knock on the door and then his key. "He's here!" she yelled. "Larry's here!"

Family came from all over the house, and they did almost knock him down. Genny and Kim shared his waist, her mother and father each had one of his arms around their shoulders, and Mac stood away, but just a few inches away, holding back a grin, not knowing exactly how to welcome his brother, man to man.

Larry called each of their names, laughing all the time as if there were something funny about them. His laughter was close to tears, and so was theirs, but nobody cried. "Ma, Kim, Genny, Pop, Mac. Mac!

Hey, I don't believe this! My kid brother's taller than I am!" He hit Mac on the arm.

"Watch it, man," Mac said, laughing then, glad to be part of the group. He helped Larry bring his bags in from the porch. Then everybody sat down.

They talked for a long time, about the army and faraway places, and about how everybody was doing in school, and about things that had happened when Genny was a baby and Kim was a smaller baby. Larry had real sideburns, and a mustache too. He was wearing jeans, not his army uniform, and once he slid further down in the green plastic lounge chair and stretched his legs out and looked slowly all around the room. Genny knew it was his way of saying it was good to be home.

After a while, Larry stood up. "Guess I'll go check out some of the brothers," he said, "see what they've been up to."

"Awww," Kim said. "Don't go yet."

"No 'aws' now, Kim," Mrs. James said in her slow way. Her round face looked a little tired.

Mr. James tightened the hand that had been resting on his knee. "Let the girl complain if she wants to, Edie," he said.

Genny saw the tiny flash of anger in her mother's eyes. Her parents were arguing about something. She didn't know what, but she knew it wasn't about what they were saying. She was glad that Larry hadn't noticed anything. She didn't want him to know how things were until after the party.

"You can go out tonight," she told him, "but not tomorrow, though."

"What's happening tomorrow?" Larry asked, moving toward the door.

"None of your business," Genny said. "It's a surprise."

*　*　*

24

They started working on the surprise early the next morning. Before Larry got up, Mr. James went to the grocery store, and when he got back they made three big bowls of tossed salad. Genny cut up tomatoes and green pepper. Kim tore up the lettuce. And Mac sliced onions with tears in his eyes.

Mr. James made piles of beef patties to cook on the grill and made two peach pies. Some of the neighbors were baking cakes, and Mrs. James made potato salad.

"Hey, what's that smelling so good down there?"

Larry's voice at the top of the stairs made Genny jump. She looked at Kim and they both ran to the stairs.

"You can't come down!" Genny said.

"What do you mean, I can't come down?" Larry said. "I have to eat breakfast, don't I?"

"No!" Kim said. "Anyway, it's lunchtime now. You can eat at the drugstore."

"Wait a minute," Larry said, "I'd better go back to the army. This family's crazy. Last night you told me I couldn't go out today, and now you're trying to kick me out. And how can I get to the drugstore if I can't come downstairs? Jump out the window?"

"Okay, come on down," Genny said. "But hold your nose. And don't look in the kitchen."

Larry held his nose and walked down the stairs like a robot, eyes straight ahead and neck stiff. At the door, he turned back with a teasing look on his face. "Man, this is going to be one bad party, uh, I mean surprise," he said.

"Just get out," Kim said. She and Genny pushed him out the door.

"Come back at four-thirty," Genny called after him. She couldn't help laugh-

ing, even though he had guessed the surprise. "Well, anyway," she told Kim, "he doesn't know where it's going to be."

"Let's make some decorations," Kim said.

"What kind?"

"I could draw a whole lot of pictures."

"Yeah!" Genny said. "And we can hang them up on Mr. Parker's clothesline."

Kim brought her drawing pad downstairs and Genny sat beside her on the floor and watched her draw. She wished she could draw pictures the way Kim could. Kim could make a lot of little lines in different colors, and when she finished, it was always a person, or a dog, or a flower, or something.

"Where did Mac go?" Genny asked her.

Kim gave her the first picture. "Down Skeeter's to get the chairs," she said.

Kim had almost enough drawings done and Genny was stacking them in a neat pile and thinking about how pretty they were going to look at the party when she heard her mother's voice upstairs.

*"Al, I tell you, I'm not going to just—"*

Her father said something back, not quite as loud, and then the door to her parents' room closed. Genny tried to hear what they were saying, but she couldn't hear very much.

Her mother said, "*You* never . . ."

And her father said, "And *you* didn't . . ."

Every time one of them said *you* like that, Genny felt as if she had been hit. She wanted somebody to really hit her so she would have a good reason to cry loud the way she wanted to and not care if Mrs. Tillman and Mike next door heard her.

Kim was still drawing, but she was making the little lines more and more slowly. Then she pushed her lips together and dropped her crayon on the coffee table. She snatched the pictures out of Genny's hand, balled them up, and threw them across the room.

Genny put her head down on the table. She heard Kim stamp up the stairs and slam her door and lock it.

"Kim?" Her father was knocking on the door. "Kim, open the door, baby."

But the door didn't open.

"Genny, where are you?" her mother called.

Genny lifted her head. "I'm downstairs," she said. She got up and sat on the sofa.

Her mother came down, frowning, and sat beside her.

"I'm sorry," her mother said. "I'm so sorry. All this yelling and screaming."

"Why do you and Daddy have to fuss all the time?" Genny said. Her mother took her hand, but Genny let her fingers stay limp.

"I . . . I don't even know, Genny," her

mother said. "We're not getting along, and every little thing seems like a big thing."

"Well, why aren't you getting along?" Genny asked. Her voice went up high and shook at the end of the question.

Mrs. James put her hand to her throat. "Genny," she said, "can we talk about it tomorrow? Let's just think about having the party. Having a good party for Larry."

Genny wanted to do that too. She said, "Okay," and when her mother went into the kitchen to start packing up the party food, she picked the pictures up off the floor and spread them out on the sofa. She ironed them with her hands the best she could.

They went to Mr. Parker's in the car, and while Mr. and Mrs. James put the food in the kitchen, Mr. Parker helped Genny. They would have to hurry back because Kim was home by herself.

Mr. Parker brought his plastic bag of

clothespins and opened out the clothesline so that it looked like an umbrella that the wind had turned inside out. He and Genny clipped the pictures to the line.

"They're kind of bent," Genny told him.

"So what?" Mr. Parker said. "A little bit of bending never hurt nothing."

When they had finished, Genny stood back and looked at the yard. Mac and his friends had set the chairs all around in small groups in front of the patches of early fall flowers and under the crape myrtle tree. The record player and the grill and the long table that would hold the food were near the porch where the shade was already beginning to push back the sun. Where the sun did remain, its touch was not heavy and glaring, but soft. And almost in the center of the yard stood the inside-out umbrella clothesline, all dressed up.

\* \* \*

UGLY. That was the first thing they saw when they walked back into the house. UGLY. Written in huge letters on Kim's drawing paper. They were all over the room—the UGLY signs—on the TV set, on the coffee table, on the sofa.

Genny couldn't move. She could only stand there in the open doorway with her mother and father and feel Kim's anger. She knew it was meant for her too, and it wasn't fair. It wasn't fair.

"Kim?" her mother called.

"Leave me alone!" Kim yelled.

Mac came up behind them in the doorway. "What's happening?" he said. Then he saw the signs. "Aw man," he said at first. And then, "I don't even feel like a party now." He came in and closed the door.

"I don't guess any of us do, Mac," Mrs. James said.

"I do!" Genny said, her voice getting loud. "I feel like having a party, and I want it to be a good party too! I don't care what Kim does!"

"Okay, baby." Her father put his arm around her. "Okay, calm down, now. We're going to have your party. Let's get dressed now and we'll all go over to Parker's and get things started. Then I'll come back here and stay with Kim." He collected the signs and carried them upstairs as if they were heavy.

Genny ignored Kim while she was getting dressed. Walked all around her. Paid no attention to her sitting on the hassock with her arms folded and her jaws puffed up like a frog. She knew Kim wanted her to say something, but she wasn't going to do it.

She was pulling her hair forward with her pick when she heard Larry come in the back door. Her mother and father and Mac had already gone, but she had waited to walk Larry over. She ran downstairs.

"Hurry up and get ready!" she said.

But Larry had a funny look on his face. "What kind of a party is this?" he said.

Genny knew without looking what Larry had seen. They hadn't thought to check the kitchen to see if Kim had put signs there too.

"The party's not here, silly," she said, trying to fake a smile. But Larry wasn't fooled. He didn't smile back.

"What's going on, Genny?" he asked.

"Kim's mad," she said.

"About what?"

Genny shrugged her shoulders. "I don't know. She's always getting mad about something."

"She didn't used to," Larry said in a quiet voice. "She upstairs?"

"Uh-huh."

It didn't take Larry long to talk Kim into

opening the door, but Genny wasn't surprised. She knew Larry could fix anything. And in a little while, they both came down, dressed for the party.

It was a quiet walk to Mr. Parker's. Quiet and comforting. Genny felt almost as if she were leaning against the arm that Larry had draped loosely around her shoulders. When they got close to the yard, somebody saw them and waved. And then people were opening the gate and calling to Larry and pulling him and shaking his hand.

Mr. James started the party off with a little speech. "This party is for Larry," he said, "to let him know how his family feels about having him home again. And . . . and how his friends feel." He was having a hard time talking, so he nodded his head once or twice and swallowed. "Well," he said finally, "everybody just . . . just have a good time. Start the music, Mac."

He gave the clothesline a hard push and it spun around, taking Kim's pictures on a

carousel ride, fast, then slower and slower, until it stopped and everybody cheered.

Talk about a party. Almost all of their friends had come, and they ate and drank and talked and danced and laughed and teased. And so did Genny. She danced with each of her brothers and with her father, and drank lemonade, and punch too, and ate three helpings of Mrs. Tillman's corn pudding, and sat on the grass at the edge of the party talking with Kim and Angela and Lynn, and teased Mac and his girl friend, and laughed. She laughed a lot for no reason. Just because.

It was a perfect party. And too soon her father was saying it was the last dance, and Genny saw Mr. Parker standing alone for a moment beside the fence and went over to dance an old-timey dance with her friend.

When bedtime finally arrived, Genny was good and ready for it. Kim was already asleep on her side of the double bed and

Genny could feel herself drifting off to the muffled sound of voices downstairs—her mother's and father's and Mac's and Larry's. Things were being worked out. She went to sleep happy, knowing that everything would be all right again in the morning.

Moving slow. Coming slow up from sleep. Leaving her party dream slow. Moving up from sleep. Slow. Kitchen dream pancake smell. Kitchen dream pancake smell. Pancake smell. Slow eyes opening. Moving. Moving fast up from sleep. Fast awake. Morning. It's morning.

*It's morning.*

Genny got up quickly. She washed up and dressed and hurried toward the pancake smell. She was the last one up. Everybody else had just about finished eating.

"I didn't want to wake you up," her mother said. "You looked so worn out."

"I did?" Genny said. "Well, I feel real good now."

"I guess you do," Mac said. "You tried to sleep for a week."

"You mean a month!" Kim said. "Hey! That reminds me of a joke. You want to hear it?"

Genny got her plate of pancakes out of the warm oven and took it to the table. She felt so good that it wasn't until she had eaten a few mouthfuls that she realized something was wrong. This breakfast wasn't like old times. Everybody was laughing and talking, but something in their voices wasn't real. Maybe they could fool Kim, but they couldn't fool her. She put her fork down.

"Something's the matter," she told them.

They looked at each other. All except Kim.

"Something's the matter," she said again. "What's the matter?"

"Why don't you finish eating, Genny?" her mother said. "We can talk about it after breakfast."

"Talk about what?" Kim asked.

Genny shoved her plate away. "I don't want my breakfast," she said.

Her mother picked up the plate and set it on top of her own. "There's something we have to tell you," she said. "Your daddy—"

Mr. James was hitting the table softly with his fist, and Genny remembered another time. The time when he had been in bed with a bad pain in his back. Genny could still see the way his fist had looked hitting the blanket over and over in that same soft way.

Something terrible was about to happen. There was only quiet at the table, and trouble.

"I'm getting a room," Mr. James said. "I'm getting a room over on Warren Street."

He said some other things too, about loving them and visiting them and taking care of them, but Genny couldn't listen. She was having a hard time hearing the words he had already said.

And then she did hear. But she didn't understand.

"You're going to *move?*" she said.

For a moment, nobody said anything. Then Kim stood up, making her chair scrape loudly as it slid back.

"I'm sorry, Daddy!" She was screaming. "I didn't mean you were ugly, I didn't mean it!"

And then her father was up too, hugging her with tears in his eyes. "No, baby, no," he said. "It's not your fault. It's me and your mama, it's our fault."

But Kim was saying over and over into his chest, "Don't leave us, Daddy, please don't leave us. I won't do it any more."

Genny turned to her mother. She was

still trying to understand. "But Larry fixed everything last night," she said.

"Genny," her mother said, "Larry couldn't—"

"But I heard him talking," Genny said. "I heard him!"

Larry shook his head slowly. "I don't know how to work magic, Genny," he said. "I wish I could, but I can't." He reached to touch her shoulder, but she leaned away.

Genny saw the hurt in his eyes and was glad. Then she saw that Mac was hurt too, for Larry, and that made her sorry. She was angry and glad and sorry, all at the same time. And mixed up. Most of all, mixed up. She wished Kim would shut up crying so she could think. Then all of a sudden she didn't want to be around any of the people in that house. She couldn't stand being around them any more.

"I'm going outside!" she said.

Standing on the porch with her arms

folded on the rail and her head on her arms, she could think. It was Larry shaking his head that had really made her angry. Shaking his head was saying no hope, no hope. But Larry could do anything, fix anything. He always used to fix her toys. And one time, he had even fixed a friendship when it was broken all to pieces. He had put her hand and Angela's together and said something crazy, and they had laughed and forgotten all about being mad. Why couldn't he do the same thing and fix her mother's and father's broken love?

In a little while, Mac came outside and stood beside her. "We're going to throw the ball around some," he said. "You want to go?"

"Is Larry going?"

"Yeah, Larry's going," Mac said, sounding mad.

"Well, I'm not going then," she said.

Mac gave her a mean look and went on

down the steps. And when Larry and Kim came out, Genny heard Larry's footsteps stop beside her for a moment, then move away. When she could no longer hear them, she turned and watched her brothers and her sister going down the street. She knew they were going over to the playground. And she knew they were taking along the red, sponge-rubber ball that they had had fun with ever since Kim was so little that she could only roll it.

But this was some old family now. Some old nothing breaking-up family. And everybody was mad. She was mad at Larry. Mac was mad at her. Kim was mad at herself. And their mother and father didn't like each other any more.

Genny sat down on the steps, but she didn't stay there long. She got up and started walking toward Sixteenth Street. She felt like talking to somebody, and there

was only one somebody she wanted to talk to. He ought to be home from church by now.

It was one of Mr. Parker's lonesome Sundays. Genny could tell as soon as she went in because he had been looking at pictures of his wife. The photo album was lying open on the sofa.

"Marlene not bringing the baby over today?" Genny asked.

Mr. Parker left the album open, but he slid it over to make room on the sofa for Genny. "She called last night," he said. "Said she was going out of town again. That's four Sundays in a row I haven't seen them. I guess my grandson will be a grown man before I get to see him again." He laughed, but it wasn't a happy laugh.

"Don't you get mad at Marlene?" Genny asked.

"I used to, Genetta," Mr. Parker said. "Used to get real mad, and hurt, too. Took me a long time to understand Marlene's giving as much as she's able to give. She's so wrapped up in her own life, her own problems, she doesn't have much left to give anybody else. I understand that now. But I still get lonesome sometimes." He touched his wife's face in the album before he closed it. "What's on your mind today?" he asked Genny.

"Can I look at the lamps?" Genny said.

"Well sure," Mr. Parker said, "if that's the way you want to spend a nice Sunday afternoon."

"I just want to see something," Genny said.

Mr. Parker led her to the room in the back that had been Marlene's when she was growing up. Now it was filled with lamps. Floor lamps standing against the wall.

Table lamps, big and little, on a two-tiered wooden table in the middle of the room. Some of them were lying down because of their broken legs. A few had already been fixed and were waiting for their owners to come and get them.

Genny looked around, then pointed to one with a big, ragged hole in the globe. "Can you fix that?" she asked.

Mr. Parker shook his head slowly the same way Larry had. "No, I sure can't," he said. "A shame, too."

"You might as well throw the lamp away, then," Genny said. Her voice sounded hard.

"Throw it away!" Mr. Parker laughed in a surprised way. "What in the world for?"

"It won't ever be the same, will it?" Genny said.

"Well, you're not the same as you were last year," Mr. Parker told her. "But we don't want to throw you away, do we? Look. I got a new globe for it. A different shape, but just as pretty, don't you think?"

"It's pretty, but—"

"But nothing!" Mr. Parker said. "This is a good lamp. The wiring is good. The switch is good. The base is strong. A good lamp." He frowned and gave Genny a close look. "I don't think we're really talking about this lamp. Are we?"

Genny didn't answer. She bit her lip and moved her shoulders up and back down again.

"Well, did I help you out any?" Mr. Parker asked.

Genny wasn't sure. "I don't know," she said. She turned to leave. It was time for her to go.

"I hope I did," Mr. Parker said. He followed her out of the room. "You sure helped me a lot. Got me to talking. Think I'll go on over to Wilson's, see if I can get him in a good argument. But you come and get me, now, if you want to talk some more."

Genny walked fast up Fletcher and across the avenue. She wanted to get to the playground before Larry and Kim and Mac left. She was still angry, but not with Larry. Not with her not-magic brother.

It was her mother and father who were giving the family a different shape, and she was angry with them. Maybe later on she would understand, the way Mr. Parker did about Marlene, but right now she didn't want to.

Genny had some thinking to do. She kept walking fast, but she slowed down her thinking. She thought about the shapes of the families she knew. Lynn lived with her mother and her grandmother. Earl and his brothers lived with their married sister. Angela and Louis lived with their mother and father and aunt and uncle and cousins.

Tony lived with his godmother and her children. Karen lived with her father and his new wife.

So many shapes. And the shapes were always changing. Somebody was born. Somebody died. Somebody moved in. Somebody moved out—the way her father was going to. Genny thought about her father going home from work and nobody being there to tell him jokes after he had taken his shower and was ready to talk. She didn't want him to be lonesome. He was still part of their family.

She said aloud, "Me and Kim and Mac and Larry and Mama. Me and Kim and Mac and Larry and Daddy." Two circles. Two circles linked together. That was their shape, for now. She would have to get used to it.

They weren't playing ball when she got to the playground. Larry and Kim were doing jumping jacks, and Mac was counting. Genny came up behind them.

"Hi," she said, but it didn't come out very loud. She said it again, and this time they turned around. They were glad to see her.

Mac had the ball. "Think quick!" he said. He threw the ball to her fast and she managed to catch it. But she didn't keep it. She threw it straight to Larry to say she was sorry.

Larry threw the ball high into the air. All four of them looked up, and all four of them put out their hands to catch it when it came back down. But they were laughing and bumping into each other, and nobody caught the ball. When it hit the ground, Mac kicked it, and they chased it across the playground.

In a little while, when they got tired of playing, they would talk. Sit on their favorite bench, the one in front of the giant stone

frog, and talk about things. About making each other feel better. About understanding, and getting used to. About fathers and mothers and families and things.

And then they would go home.

ELOISE GREENFIELD is the author of thirteen books for children, including *She Come Bringing Me That Little Baby Girl*, which won the Irma Simonton Black Award in 1974. The Council on Interracial Books for Children has cited her for her contributions to the field of children's literature. Ms. Greenfield lives with her husband in Washington, D.C.

JAMES CALVIN is a young artist and designer who has illustrated several books and magazine stories and has done many paintings for book jackets. Mr. Calvin lives and works in New York.